PIERRE

a cautionary tale

PIERRE AND HIS PARENTS

PIERRE

a cautionary tale

IN
FIVE CHAPTERS
AND A
PROLOGUE

MAURICE SENDAK

SCHOLASTIC BOOK SERVICES
NEW YORK · TORONTO · LONDON · AUCKLAND · SYDNEY · TOKYO

ISBN: 0-590-31945-0

Copyright © 1962 by Maurice Sendak. This edition is published by Scholastic Book Services, a division of Scholastic Magazines, Inc., by arrangement with Harper & Row, Publishers, Inc.

13 12 11 10 9 8 7 6   0/8

Printed in the U.S.A.

TABLE OF CONTENTS

PROLOGUE

There once was a boy
named Pierre
who only would say,
"I don't care!"
Read his story,
my friend,
for you'll find
at the end
that a suitable
moral lies there.

7

CHAPTER 1

One day
his mother said
when Pierre
climbed out of bed,
"Good morning,
darling boy,
you are
my only joy."
Pierre said,
"I don't care!"

"What would you
like to eat?"
"I don't care!"
"Some lovely
cream of wheat?"
"I don't care!"
"Don't sit backwards
on your chair."
"I don't care!"
"Or pour syrup
on your hair."
"I don't care!"

"You are acting
like a clown."
"*I don't care!*"
"And we have
to go to town."
"*I don't care!*"
"Don't you want
to come, my dear?"
"*I don't care!*"
"Would you rather
stay right here?"
"*I don't care!*"

So his mother
left him there.

CHAPTER 2

His father said,
"Get off your head
or I will march you
up to bed!"
Pierre said,
"I don't care!"
"I would think
that you could see—"
"I don't care!"
"Your head is where
your feet should be!"
"I don't care!"

"If you keep standing
upside down—"
"*I don't care!*"
"We'll never ever
get to town."
"*I don't care!*"
"If only you would
say I CARE."
"*I don't care!*"
"I'd let you fold
the folding chair."
"*I don't care!*"

So his parents
left him there.
They didn't take him
anywhere.

CHAPTER 3

Now, as the night
began to fall
a hungry lion
paid a call.
He looked Pierre
right in the eye
and asked him
if he'd like to die.
Pierre said,
"I don't care!"

"I can eat you,
don't you see?"
"I don't care!"
"And you will be
inside of me."
"I don't care!"
"Then you'll never
have to bother—"
"I don't care!"
"With a mother
and a father."
"I don't care!"

"Is that all
you have to say?"
"*I don't care!*"
"Then I'll eat you,
if I may."
"*I don't care!*"

So the lion
ate Pierre.

CHAPTER 4

Arriving home
at six o'clock,
his parents had
a dreadful shock!
They found the lion
sick in bed
and cried,
"Pierre is surely dead!"

They pulled the lion
by the hair.
They hit him
with the folding chair.
His mother asked,
"Where is Pierre?"
The lion answered,
"I don't care!"
His father said,
"Pierre's in there!"

CHAPTER 5

They rushed the lion
into town.
The doctor shook him
up and down.
And when the lion
gave a roar—
Pierre fell out
upon the floor.
He rubbed his eyes
and scratched his head
and laughed
because he wasn't dead.
His mother cried
and held him tight.

His father asked,
"Are you all right?"
Pierre said,
"I am feeling fine,
please take me home,
it's half past nine."
The lion said,
"If you would care
to climb on me,
I'll take you there."
Then everyone
looked at Pierre
who shouted,
"Yes, indeed I care!!"

The lion took them
home to rest
and stayed on
as a weekend guest.

The moral of Pierre
is: CARE!